We are the Dino Diggers – the best in Dino-Tow...
We put things right when they go wrong and never let you down.

For Austin – R.I.

BLOOMSBURY CHILDREN'S BOOKS
Bloomsbury Publishing Plc
50 Bedford Square, London, WC1B 3DP, UK

BLOOMSBURY, BLOOMSBURY CHILDREN'S BOOKS and the Diana logo are trademarks of Bloomsbury Publishing Plc

First published in Great Britain 2018 by Bloomsbury Publishing Plc

ISBN: PB: 978 1 4088 7248 2; eBook: 978 1 4088 7247 5

2 4 6 8 10 9 7 5 3 1

Printed in China by Leo Paper Products, Heshan, Guangdong

All papers used by Bloomsbury Publishing Plc are natural, recyclable products from
wood grown in well managed forests. The manufacturing processes conform to
the environmental regulations of the country of origin

To find out more about our authors and books visit www.bloomsbury.com and sign up for our newsletters

Dumper Truck Danger

Rose Impey   Chris Chatterton

BLOOMSBURY
CHILDREN'S BOOKS
LONDON OXFORD NEW YORK NEW DELHI SYDNEY

Today, despite the stormy weather, the Dino Diggers are having a big clear-up.

Tyrone T. rex is helping Stacey Stegosaurus fill her dumper truck.

All the spare rocks are going to the Dino-Town Garden Centre.

Dino Diggers Inc.

Stacey sets off to deliver them.

"Hurry back," Terri Dactyl tells her.
"There's lots more work to do."

"No worries," says Stacey.

But, on the way, Stacey is waved down by a very worried-looking Mrs Silvi Saurus, the mayor of Dino-Town.

"Stop! Stop!" she says. "Something terrible has happened."

"It's the town bridge," she explains.
"It's collapsed in this storm and
taken the baker's van with it!"

This is bad news, thinks Stacey.
Without a bridge Dino-Town will be cut off.
Luckily, she knows exactly who to call.

"Leave this to us," she tells the mayor.
"You know our motto."

When the Dino Diggers reach the river they see that most of the bridge has been completely washed away. And poor Di Ceretops, the Dino-Town baker, is trapped in his van which keeps sinking further into the mud.

"Please, can't someone help me?" he calls.

"This is a Dino-Town Tragedy!"
says Terri.

But while Terri is still working
out what to do, Tyrone
jumps into his digger.
"I'll soon fix this," he says.
"I've got a plan."

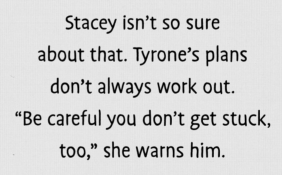

Stacey isn't so sure
about that. Tyrone's plans
don't always work out.
"Be careful you don't get stuck,
too," she warns him.

"With these wheels?"
Tyrone laughs.
"Not a chance."

Tyrone drives straight into the soft mud,
which makes a loud sucking sound.

But Tyrone presses on, scooping up mud as he goes, and emptying the shovel behind him.

SCHLUKKK!

His digger is working as hard as it possibly can to clear a path to Di Ceretops's van.

SCHLUKKK!

At last, with one final effort, Tyrone reaches him and starts to push them both onto safer ground.

All the Dino Diggers have watched the big rescue.
Tyrone is feeling very proud of himself, until . . .
OH NO,
he suddenly realises they are both on the wrong side
of the bridge. How will they ever get back?

This time Stacey has a plan –
but it could be a dangerous one.

Very slowly, Stacey expertly backs her dumper truck
right to the very edge of the broken bridge.
"Hang on there, Tyrone," she calls.
"Remember our motto: Dino Diggers never let you down.
And we never let each other down either."

With great skill, Stacey carefully dumps
all her rocks into the muddy riverbed.

It may be a bit bumpy, but now Tyrone
and Di Ceretops have a safe way to drive out.

"That was a clever plan of yours," Terri tells Stacey.
And Tyrone agrees. "She saved us all. Hooray for Stacey!"

"What a tremendous team," says Terri.
"Now everyone back to work. Let's get this bridge fixed!"

When Mrs Silvi Saurus officially opens the new bridge the traffic pours across.

"Three cheers for the Dino Diggers," she calls.
And all the traffic honks its horns in agreement.

Hooray for the Dino Diggers, another job well done!
Here are other stories full of Dino-Digging fun.

Digger Disaster

Crane Calamity

Dumper Truck Danger